Contents

Coach

Left Full
Back

Midfield
(Centre)

Striker

Goalkeeper

Right Full
Back

Centre
Back

Kirsten
Browne

Barry 'Bazza'
Watts

Daisy
Higgins

Colin 'Colly'
Flower

Tarlock
Bhasin

Lennie
Gould
(captain)

Trev the
Rev

Substitute

Midfield
(Centre)

Centre
Back

Substitute

Midfield
(Right)

Striker

Midfield
(Left)

Mick
Ryall

Jonjo
Rix

Lulu
Squibb

Jeremy
Emery

Rhoda
O'Neill

Lionel
Murgatroyd

Ricky
King

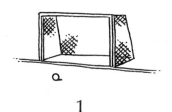

1

Butterfingers Browne!

Kirsten Browne, Angels FC's goalkeeper, knocked the drip off the end of her nose with the back of her glove.

Her hair looked like soggy spaghetti. Her football gear was dribbling more than the trickiest winger. The ground around her looked like a sea of brown jelly and, when she tried to lift her feet, sounded like it too. Squelch, squelch.

"Not much fun being a goalie, eh?" said a voice.

Kirsten risked a quick look round, although she knew exactly who had spoken. 'Cap Man,' was her name for him. He was a tall man, never without his flat cap and walking stick, who regularly stopped to watch the Angels' matches.

"It is when you're winning a cup match!" replied Kirsten cheerfully.

And the Angels were winning, 1-0, against Harnett Rovers.

"Although it's more like a bucket match than a cup match," muttered Kirsten to herself as she turned back to the game.

The rain had been pouring down for the past two days and the pitch was in a dreadful state. Even the Angels' goal, scored by their midfielder Micky Ryall, had been a bit of a fluke. His shot had been going wide when it had hit a large blob of mud and changed direction to whistle into the Harnett net.

Kirsten shook her drenched hair like a dog sending spray everywhere. Still, there couldn't be more than a couple of minutes left. All they had to do was hang on to their lead and she'd soon be back in the warm, dry changing room celebrating their victory.

"Ginger's ball!"

Kirsten heard the sudden screech before she spotted the danger coming her way. Harnett's star player, a fiery ginger-headed boy with amazingly baggy shorts, had slipped the ball to a team-mate and was splashing through a gap in the Angels' defence as he screamed for the return pass.

It came, the perfect one-two. Ginger was through, and racing her way!

"Go to meet him!" said the voice from behind her goal.

Kirsten splurged forward through the muddy goalmouth - then stopped. What was she doing? What did Cap Man know about goalkeeping? He didn't look as though he could tell one end of a football boot from the other.

Besides, the Angels' right back, Bazza Watts, was covering the move. Cap Man obviously hadn't seen him. So much for touchline experts! Kirsten stayed put, confident that Bazza had it all under control.

Unfortunately, Bazza didn't even have his own feet under control. Realising that he'd got his angle of approach all wrong, the Angels' player tried to change direction. It was a disaster. Bazza's feet went one way but his body went the other. As the full-back dived into the mud like a hippopotamus on holiday, Ginger raced on into the penalty area.

This time, Kirsten did go to meet him.

She'd lost a valuable couple of seconds
though, and it made all the difference.
Instead of reaching Ginger in time to whip
the ball off his toe, she was a fraction late.
He got to it first and toe-poked the ball past
her - only to slip over himself! Desperately,
Kirsten swung round. A metre away the
Harnett player was on the ground, sliding
head-first towards the ball in a mess of mud
and water. It was her chance! If she could
only dive and get that ball...

Kirsten launched herself towards it. Splosh! Mud shot up everywhere as she landed. But, even as she closed her eyes, Kirsten thrust her hands out - and grabbed the ball! She'd done it! The firm, round shape was in her hands!

What's more, the referee's whistle was shrieking for full-time. Or was it? The whistle had only gone *peep!* instead of the usual up-and-down *pee-ya-peep!* that signalled the end of a game. But what else could it be blowing for?

Even as she wondered, other confusing questions crowded into her mind. What was Ginger yelling about? And, most confusing of all, why was the ball in her hands moving?

Kirsten blinked her eyes open - and groaned. There was a round, firm shape in her hands all right. Unfortunately, it wasn't a football! Footballs didn't have ginger hair.

And they definitely didn't shout "Penalty, Ref!"at the tops of their voices.

In her headlong dive she hadn't grabbed the ball. She'd swooped and grabbed Ginger's head!

"Penalty!" The referee had hared up and was pointing to the spot.

All around her, Kirsten heard the wails of agony from the Angels players.

"A penalty?" cried Tarlock Bhasin. "That's it, then!"

"They can't miss," moaned Lulu Squibb.

"It must be a goal," groaned Jeremy Emery.

All the other Angels players simply sighed hopelessly. Trudging back into her goal, Kirsten knew why. It was because never, ever, in her goalkeeping career had she saved a penalty kick. She'd never even got near to saving one. For some reason, she always guessed the wrong way to dive.

Planting her feet firmly on her goal-line Kirsten crouched, like a determined question mark. In front of her, Ginger had

14

miraculously recovered and was plonking the ball down on the penalty spot. He was going to take the kick himself.

"Get your weight on your left foot," said a quiet voice from behind Kirsten's goal. "That's the way he'll put it. To your left."

To her left! Kirsten flicked an angry glance in Cap Man's direction. What did he know? He didn't look as if he could stop a bottle with a cork!

She turned back to face Ginger. To my right, decided Kirsten, I'll go to my right. Ginger's right-footed, so that's where he'll put the kick. To put it the other way would mean him having to side-foot the ball. In this mud - he won't chance it. To her left, indeed!

Shifting her weight firmly onto her right foot, Kirsten got ready to spring. She was already leaning well to her right as Ginger ran in. The moment he struck the ball, she dived headlong - only to see the ball trickle gently into the opposite corner of the goal.

Cap Man had been right. And she'd guessed wrong again.

"Bad luck, Kirsten," said Lennie Gould, the Angels' captain, as they trudged back into the changing rooms. "Anyone can make a mistake."

"Yeah," nodded Jonjo Rix seriously. "Easy done. Okay, so heads do have things like ears and noses and eyes and mouths…"

"And ginger hair," chipped in Rhoda O'Neill.

"Right. But apart from that lot - man, a

head looks just like a football!"

"Not!" yelled everybody else in unison.

"Okay, okay." It was Trevor Rowe, the Angels' coach. A hush fell over the room. When Trev spoke, everybody listened. "Look on the bright side. A draw means we're still in the cup. We'll just have to win next Saturday's replay."

"What if it's a draw again?" asked 'Colly' Flower, the team's striker.

"Then there'll be a penalty shoot-out to decide the winners," said Trev.

Everybody looked Kirsten's way. Her heart sank. A penalty shoot-out! If it came to that, the Angels would have no chance.

Unless, that is, she could come up with a plan.

A powerful, penalty-saving plan ...

2

Practice Makes...Perfectly Awful!

Practice, that was what Kirsten decided she needed after some serious thought: penalty-saving practice, and lots of it. The others would help her, surely.

She picked up the telephone next morning. She would start at the top, with Lennie Gould, the team's captain and chief penalty-taker.

"Lennie, it's Kirsten. How about getting down to Youth Club an hour early tonight and giving me some penalty-saving practice?"

All the Angels players were members of St Jude's Youth Club. The hall they used was next door to St. Jude's Church, and there was a perfect strip of grass which ran between the two buildings.

"Er ... I'm not sure." Lennie sounded doubtful.

"Lennie, I need the practice!" Kirsten shouted into the telephone. "I've got to get better at saving penalties!"

"Yeah, but ... that's it," said Lennie. "What if you actually saved one of mine while we were practising? Then I'd get worried. I could lose my penalty-taking confidence."

"You wouldn't."

"I would. No, it's too risky. I'm going to spend the week practising against a wall. Sorry."

Kirsten rang Colin 'Colly' Flower, the team's ace striker. He made the same excuse. So did Daisy Higgins when Kirsten rang her. And Jonjo Rix. And Mick Ryall. And the rest of the team. None of the Angels players wanted to take the chance of having their confidence destroyed through Kirsten saving one of their penalty kicks.

"Lionel," sighed Kirsten, dialling one last number. "It'll just have to be Lionel."

Lionel Murgatroyd was the Angels' regular substitute, for the simple reason that his ability didn't match his enthusiasm. The only chance Lionel had of getting in the team would be for somebody to break their leg between now and the game.

"Well...all right," said Lionel when Kirsten got through to him. "But I'm not very good, you know that."

Youth Club began at 6.30 pm. It was just before 5.30 that Kirsten arrived. Lionel was already waiting, his football boots slung over his shoulder. Together they pushed through the door - only to meet Trev.

"You two are early," he smiled. "The clocks didn't go forward last night, y'know."

Kirsten explained. "This is dedication to goalkeeping duty, Trev. Good old Lionel's going to give me an hour's penalty practice on the grass outside."

Trev shook his head. "No he isn't, Kirsten. Not in this weather. Your parents expect me to send you home from Youth Club looking pretty much the same way you arrived - which isn't going to be the case if you spend an hour playing out there."

"N. O. No!" said Trev. "Look, I've got some work to do before the others turn up. Settle down in the meetings room, eh? If you're lucky you'll find some tasty left-overs in there. One of the parishioners used it for a children's party yesterday."

Glumly, Kirsten led the way to the meetings room. This was a small, comfortable room next to the main hall they used for the Youth Club. It was set out just like a living-room with comfy armchairs, a sideboard, coffee tables, a standard lamp, balloons…

Balloons? Kirsten stopped as she opened the meetings room door. Of course, the children's party. On the sideboard there was still a large jug of orange juice and various crispy morsels in dishes.

But it was the balloons that gave Kirsten the idea. "Lionel," she said, "I reckon it's practice time!"

"Uh?" said Lionel. "I thought Trev said no playing outside."

"He did. But he didn't say we couldn't play inside, did he? We can practise in here!"

"In here?" Lionel gazed around the room. "What if we smash something? Football's are hard, y'know."

"But balloons aren't, are they?" Kirsten snatched up the balloon she'd spotted. "We

can't break anything with a balloon! And it'll dip and curve in the air, so it'll be an even better test for my reflexes."

Quickly Kirsten opened the curtains at the end of the room. "The curtains are the goalposts," she said.

She then shoved the armchairs and coffee table to one side, clearing a space in the middle of the room. "One penalty area," she said. Finally, she spread a row of cushions on the floor to dive on. "And one goal-line! Come on, Lionel, penalty time!"

"Are you sure about this?"

"Of course I'm sure," said Kirsten. Pacing as far as she could from her cushion goal-line, she plonked the balloon on a flowery blob of carpet. "That's the penalty spot. It's not the right distance, but it doesn't matter. Balloons don't fly as far as footballs because they're all soft and squashy. That's why there's nothing to worry about, Lionel."

"O-kay," said Lionel. "Get ready."

Taking a step backwards, Lionel ran in uncertainly. He was never too sure where a football would go when he kicked it, and he was even less sure about a balloon.

BOP!

As it happened, he struck it well. The balloon shot off towards the left-hand side of the curtains.

Kirsten, true to form, went the wrong way.

Even as she did so, and the balloon slapped against the window for a 'goal', another bright idea whizzed into Kirsten's mind. If her diabolical guessing meant she'd always go the wrong way, perhaps the answer was to practice mid-air changes of direction. And what better time than now?

As the balloon sank to the floor, Kirsten did just that. Twisting in the air, she turned back and leapt on top of it.

Bang!

It was the unexpected suddenness of the sound that did it, coming just as Lionel was breathing a sigh of relief that he'd managed to kick the balloon straight and not hit anything. Startled, he threw up an arm and knocked over the standard lamp.

The lamp toppled over. Its shade flew off and slid the length of the sideboard before clattering into the jug of left-over orange juice. The jug took off. The orange juice cascaded out. And Kirsten, still on the floor directly beneath it, got drowned.

"You couldn't have got much damper if I had let you play outside," said Trev from the doorway.

"I only want to get better at facing penalties," said Kirsten. She was sitting beside the radiator in Trev's study. No longer damp, she was now extremely sticky. "I was thinking of the team."

"I don't know that having you wreck the Youth Club is a price worth paying," said Trev.

"How do I get better then? Got any suggestions?"

Trev looked thoughtful. "Possibly…"

Kirsten leapt to her feet. "What? I'll try anything!"

"Anything?"

"Yes! Yes! Anything at all!"

Trev picked up the phone. "Right. I know that Des Young, one of our parishioners, needs someone to do a little bit of work for him. If you're game, I think I could talk him into giving you some goalkeeping lessons in return."

"Really!" squealed Kirsten. "Is he a goalie, then?"

"Was," said Trev. "A good one, too."

"Ring him up then, Trev. Tell him he's got some help. Kirsten the Kat is on the way!"

3

This Little Piggy…

Wednesday after school found Kirsten hurrying excitedly away from the main road and up towards the top of the hill which was just visible from St Jude's. It had been a rush to get home and changed out of her school uniform, but she'd managed it.

"Old clothes," Trev had said after sorting out the arrangements with his Des Young person. "Wear something that can get dirty - but not your football kit."

Kirsten shrugged. Odd, but who was she to argue? She'd wear a clown's outfit complete with red nose if she ended up a better goalkeeper!

She found the cottage she was looking for halfway up the hill. It was small and square, with a large patch of land at the side. Kirsten ran up and rattled at the door.

Des Young, goalkeeper. What would he look like? she wondered. Tall and wide, probably, with a face that said: "put one past me if you dare!"

The cottage door swung open - and so did Kirsten's mouth. The man in front of her was tall all right. He was quite wide too. What she hadn't expected was that he'd also be wearing a cap and be holding a walking-stick. It was Cap Man!

Kirsten was still struggling to overcome her surprise, even after Des Young had said hello and started to explain what he wanted her to do.

"I've got five little 'uns I need some help with. Their mum's not too well, and so I've got to give 'em their meals myself."

Five little 'uns? Meals? Surely he doesn't want me to do the cooking while his wife's in bed!

Des Young hadn't finished, though. "Trouble is, I'm not too quick on my feet any more," he said, patting his leg. "So I have a bit of trouble rounding them up. That's where you come in, Kirsten. You catch the little rascals for me, and I'll feed 'em."

Rounding up his five children? Was that all? A couple of quick shouts and it would be done. "Fine," said Kirsten. "What are their names?"

"Annie, Wilbur, Buzz, Ruby and Nipper. Nipper's the troublesome one."

"Indoors, are they?"

Des Young frowned and shook his head. "No. They're round the back. Come on, I'll show you."

Kirsten followed him round behind the cottage to where, she was surprised to discover, there was quite a bit more land on which various crops were growing. A section near the cottage had been fenced off, though. Des Young clicked open a gate

leading into this yard and led the way
across to a square brick shed.

"There you go," he said as they reached
it, "all five of 'em are in there."

"In there?" Kirsten could hardly believe
her eyes. The shed was filthy - and it didn't
smell too good, either. "You let your
children play in there!"

"My children?" Des Young smiled, then
broke into a loud laugh. "Kirsten," he said
as reached down and took hold of the
shed's wooden door, "I think there's been

some misunderstanding. Meet Annie, Wilbur, Buzz, Ruby and Nipper!"

He slid the door back. Immediately, what looked like five different-coloured blurs with curly tails shot out and began racing around like mad.

"Piglets!" cried Kirsten.

"Right," said Des Young. "You catch 'em, and then I'll feed 'em from a bottle."

"What about the goalkeeper training?"

"Not until they've all been caught and fed. Especially that one. That's Nipper."

Four of the blurs had stopped running and were now sniffing around but the fifth, the one Des Young was pointing at, was still on the move. Careering around the yard like a bundle of brown and white lightning, it was all Kirsten could do to keep an eye on it.

"No problem," she said. "I'll leave him till last. Let him tire himself out."

"Fine. I'll be indoors. Every time you catch one, bring it over." Des Young walked stiffly back towards the cottage. He stopped at the fence. "Oh, yes. Whatever you do, don't forget to shut this gate. Leave it open and Nipper will go for it like a bullet. He'll be down to that main road before you know it and that'll be that. Bacon for tea."

As he disappeared into the cottage, Kirsten looked around the yard. This was going to be easy. She'd be practising penalty saves in no time at all.

It wasn't that easy, though. Her early attempts at piglet-catching left her empty-handed as Annie accelerated or Buzz buzzed or Wilbur wiggled or Ruby raced away. Gradually, though, Kirsten got the idea. Waiting until they found some interesting morsel on the ground, she'd tiptoe up behind them and grab them quickly.

"Only Nipper to go now,"

she said confidently as she brought Ruby in for Des Young to place on his knee and feed with a baby's bottle of milk. "Back in a minute."

In the yard, Nipper had finally stopped running around. Kirsten crept towards him. Nipper gazed up at her, looking as if he was grinning from ear to ear.

Easy, she thought. He's as tired as a full-back who's just spent ninety minutes facing Ryan Giggs. Closer and closer she crept until she was just a few metres away.

That was when Nipper took off, racing straight towards her. Kirsten moved into position to stop him. Too late. Before she'd even bent her knees the piglet had changed

direction and shot past her like a bullet.

Kirsten turned to face him again. He was laughing from ear to ear, she was sure he was! Right. This was going to be it. Crouching low, she shuffled slowly towards Nipper. Again he took off, straight towards her.

The dumb animal will do the same as last time, reckoned Kirsten. This time as the piglet drew near she launched herself into a dive, only to land in something very smelly as Nipper shot by on the other side.

Little had changed an hour later. As Des Young strolled out from the cottage, Nipper was still on the loose.

"Having trouble?"

"Yes, I am!" snapped Kirsten who was by this time feeling very hot and even smellier.

Des Young eased open the gate. "Here, let me show you how."

You are joking! Kirsten thought. If I can't catch him, what chance have you got? She stood back and watched.

Just as she had, Des Young crept closer to Nipper, crouching as he moved. But then, instead of getting nearer, he stopped 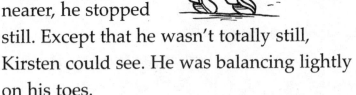 still. Except that he wasn't totally still, Kirsten could see. He was balancing lightly on his toes.

Suddenly, Nipper did his party trick. Bursting forward, he ran straight towards

Des Young. But the tall man didn't dive.
Keeping his eyes fixed firmly on the
rocketing piglet, he waited to see which way
Nipper was going to go. Then he dived,
clutching the squealing piglet in his huge
hands.

"Very good," said Kirsten irritably. She
followed Des Young as he carried Nipper
into the cottage's small kitchen.

"So, goalie training next is it?" she asked
as he settled the piglet on his knee.

Des Young looked at his watch. "It
would have been if you'd caught Nipper
quickly. It's got a bit too late now."

Too late? Kirsten felt as if steam was

coming out of her ears. "It wouldn't be too late if you'd come out and caught him an hour ago!" she yelled.

"Look, can you come back Saturday morning? Before your match?"

"And go out on the pitch smelling all horrible? My defenders would conk out!"

"No pig-catching. I promise."

But Kirsten wasn't in a mood to calm down. She'd come here for goalkeeper-training and all she'd been given was the run-around by five little pigs.

"I bet you don't know anything about goalkeeping! I bet you don't know the difference between a penalty spot and a spot on the end of your nose!"

Calmly, Des Young reached to open a cabinet drawer. He took out a small, flat box and handed it to Kirsten.

"Have a look at that when you get home," he said. "Maybe that'll give you more faith in me. You can bring it back with you on Saturday morning."

"If I come!" yelled Kirsten, slamming the door as she marched out.

44

4

Give her a Medal!

By the time she got home, Kirsten had
cooled down a bit. She was also wondering
what Des Young had given her to look at.

Sitting on her bed, she opened the box.
Inside, lying on a cushion of velvet, was a
medal. Kirsten looked - and looked again.

"It's an FA Cup Winner's medal," she
gasped. Turning it over, she looked at the
date on the back. Then, rushing for her well-
thumbed football encyclopaedia containing
every fact a football fanatic could wish to
know, she riffled through the pages.

There it was, for the year stamped on the medal. The Cup-winning team. Goalkeeper: D. Young. It was just incredible. She, Kirsten Browne, had met a man who'd climbed the steps to the Royal Box at Wembley.

The next moment she groaned loudly. What had she told him? That she didn't think he knew anything about goalkeeping! That on Saturday morning she might, just might turn up to be trained by him!

Might? Nothing could stop her going back there now!

It had seemed like the longest week ever. Time and again Kirsten had gazed at Des Young's medal and wondered if Saturday would ever come.

She was still looking at it as she reached

the bottom of the hill leading up to his cottage, which was why she didn't notice the two boys until they cycled up on either side of her.

"Hey, Brett! Look who it isn't! An Angel. Where's your wings, Angel?"

"She must have lost 'em, Ginger. That's why she always flies the wrong way!"

Kirsten whirled round. It was Ginger, the Harnett team's star. The other boy, Brett Thompson, Kirsten recognised as their substitute.

"So, what's this, Angel?"

Before Kirsten knew it, Ginger had snatched the medal from her hand.

"Give it back."

"Wow! A Cup-winner's medal. Where'd you get it?"

"From a man named Des Young. He was a top goalie. I'm taking it back to him now. He's going to give me some coaching…"

Kirsten knew she'd made a mistake the moment she said it. Tossing the medal to his mate, Ginger yelled, "Go, Brett!"

As his pal raced off, Ginger grinned at Kirsten. "You can have it back after the game, Angel. On one condition."

"What condition?"

"Simple," said Ginger. "Do the same as last week and give us a penalty."

"On purpose?" cried Kirsten.

"You've got it," said Ginger. "Brett will be on the touch-line with that medal. When I bang in the penalty, you'll get it back. Right?"

"And if I say no?"

"No penalty, no medal," laughed Ginger, riding off. "See you at the game!"

Kirsten watched him go. What could she do? Without doing what he wanted, she wouldn't get Des Young's medal back. And without that medal she couldn't - she just couldn't - turn up to see him this morning.

She'd just turned round to begin walking home when she heard a shout.

"Kirsten! Stop him!"

Kirsten swung round. The shout had come from Des Young. He was at the far end of the lane. And racing towards her, his little legs whizzing round like Catherine wheels, was Nipper.

"Oh, no! He must have left the gate open!"

If he got past her, Nipper would be at the main road. She had to stop him! Desperately, she tried to remember how Des had done it.

Balanced lightly on his toes for a start, something she'd never done. Kirsten lifted her heels and immediately felt the difference it made. Then, as Nipper came rocketing towards her, she crouched low and kept her eyes fixed on him just as Des Young had done.

Closer and closer he got. Still Kirsten didn't move. Only when she saw Nipper dart to one side did she take a flying leap.

Both her hands closed over the little pink body. Nipper squealed and wriggled. She'd caught him!

Des Young came hurrying down the lane towards her. "Brilliant, Kirsten. I'm glad you turned up after all."

"Er…" stammered Kirsten. What could she do now? She couldn't possibly tell him about the medal. "I…I only came to say I couldn't come, if you know what I mean. And…I've forgotten your medal, I'm afraid. I'll bring it back after the match."

Handing over the wriggling Nipper before Des Young could say a word, Kirsten raced off.

If she was going to get his medal back, she had some serious thinking to do before the match began.

5

Remember Nipper!

Ginger and Brett sidled up to her as the teams filed out onto the pitch.

"Remember, Angel," whispered Ginger, threateningly. "No penalty…"

"No medal…" said Brett the substitute, patting the pocket of his tracksuit top.

"What did Ginger want?" asked Bazza Watts as the two Harnett players sprinted off. "Asking you to leave his head alone this time was he?"

"Asking her to grab it, more like," said Daisy Higgins. "He scored from the penalty, remember."

Jonjo Rix looked at Kirsten. "Repeat after me: footballs do not have ginger hair, footballs do not have ginger hair…"

"All right," said Kirsten. "If you bang in a dozen goals it won't matter, will it?"

But, as she took her place in goal, she knew that wasn't likely. Like the first match, this one was going to be a tight game. A penalty could make all the difference.

So it proved. The two teams were evenly matched and the first half ended without either team having had any real scoring chances.

"I can see this coming to a penalty shoot-out," said Colly Flower glumly.

"Me too," said Rhoda O'Neill.

Kirsten knew what they were thinking, because she was thinking the same. Balloon practice, pig practice - her plans had ended in disaster. On top of everything, there was Des Young's medal and Ginger's threat. She knew what she had to do. The question was: how?

The second half began. A quick Harnett raid was ended by Kirsten whipping the ball off the end of Ginger's toe. "No penalty..." he murmured as he ran back.

Kirsten pretended not to hear. She threw the ball out to Tarlock Bhasin. Playing a quick one-two with Daisy Higgins, Tarlock took the ball as far as the half-way line before releasing it to Colly Flower. As Colly looked around, apparently unsure who to pass to, Tarlock kept going. It was a great tactic. Colly switched direction and hammered the ball to the unmarked Tarlock who raced on down to the byline before pulling the ball back for Jonjo Rix to bang into the roof of the net. 1-0 to the Angels!

Everybody except Kirsten jumped for joy. All she could think about was Des Young's medal and how she was going to get it back.

The game restarted, but the Angels were playing really well. So many Harnett attacks were being broken down that Kirsten was almost a spectator. With only a few minutes left, she'd had no chance to do what she planned to do.

Out on the touchline, Harnett were preparing to bring on their substitute in a last-gasp effort to save the game. Brett Thompson was running down the touchline to warm up.

Suddenly, Harnett broke away, Ginger racing on to a long ball over Bazza Watts' head. It was the chance Kirsten had been waiting for. As Bazza turned to give chase, Kirsten raced from her goal.

"Penalty, Angel!" yelled Ginger as, with Bazza right behind him, he hared into the penalty box.

But Kirsten had her plan, and it didn't include doing what he wanted. Reaching the ball first, she hammered it hard and low off the pitch - straight into Brett Thompson's stomach! As he collapsed in a heap, and Ginger did the same thing behind her, Kirsten raced off the pitch.

"Poor Brett," she cried, bending down, "are you all right?"

"Shove...off!" gasped the substitute. "You did that...on purpose!"

"Too right," said Kirsten, whipping the FA Cup medal out of his pocket. "It worked, as well!"

"Do you want me to take that?"

As she turned to see Des Young, Kirsten nodded dumbly. He must have been watching all the time.

"Thanks," he said as Kirsten handed it over. "Now, you go and save that penalty."

"Penalty? What penalty?"

"Your full-back reached that ginger-headed lad just as you whacked the ball into touch. Didn't touch him, but he leapt into the air as if he'd been kicked by an elephant. Fooled the referee, too. He's given a penalty."

Kirsten turned back to the match. Ginger was busy putting the ball on the spot.

"If only I'd got that coaching from you," she wailed.

Des Young grinned. "But you did," he said. "How did you catch Nipper? Stayed on your toes, kept your eyes on him and moved when you saw which way he was going. If that's not goalkeeping I don't know what is! Go on, get in that goal and do the same!"

Kirsten went back to stand on her goal-line.

She bounced on her toes, instead of standing flat-footed.

As Ginger ran in, she didn't look at him. Instead, just as she had with Nipper, she kept her eyes glued to the ball until she saw which way it was going.

Only then did Kirsten leap that way - the right way - to snaffle the ball with both hands! She'd saved it!

"Well done," said Des Young as the Angels ran out 1-0 winners.

Kirsten beamed. "Thanks to you. I wish you'd told me Nipper-chasing was goal-keeper training. I wouldn't have got so annoyed."

"Sorry about that. I was going to tell you on Saturday morning, but you rushed off too quickly."

"I didn't want to tell you about your medal."

"I wouldn't have minded," said Des Young.

"Wouldn't have minded!" cried Kirsten. "I imagined you'd go bananas! If I won a

Cup Final medal I wouldn't let it out of my sight!"

The ex-goalkeeper grinned. "Me neither." He pulled the medal he'd loaned to Kirsten from his pocket. "That's why I had this copy made. The real one's at home, safe and sound!"